THREE CHORDS AND A BEAT

by Chris Everheart

www.12StoryLibrary.com

Copyright © 2015 by Peterson Publishing Company, North Mankato, MN 56003. All rights reserved. No part of this book may be reproduced or utilized in any form or by any means without written permission from the publisher.

12-Story Library is an imprint of Peterson Publishing Company and Press Room Editions.

Produced for 12-Story Library by Red Line Editorial

Photographs ©: Shutterstock Images, cover, 3

Cover Design: Jake Nordby

ISBN
978-1-63235-058-9 (hardcover)
978-1-63235-118-0 (paperback)
978-1-62143-099-5 (hosted ebook)

Library of Congress Control Number: 2014945999

Printed in the United States of America
Mankato, MN
October, 2014

CHAPTER
1

Trey died six months ago, on a normal
Saturday afternoon. The sun was shining.
His car rattled when it rolled down the street.
And we had an argument at the mall. Nothing
out of the norm for us—except the dying part.
He wasn't supposed to die that day.

We'd gotten to the mall around 3:00. Mom
made him take me along because she was sick
of me moping around the house. I was being a
grouch, she said, and a little fresh air would do
me good. I wasn't convinced, and Trey wasn't
excited about taking me with him. He was going
to the food court to see his girlfriend, so he didn't
want me hanging around.

That suited me fine. As soon as we got there, I peeled off and slipped into the discount shoe store. He went to make eyes at his girl, Jayna, and I tried on a bunch of high-tops. I really wanted the pair with gold stripes and a red tongue. But I put them back on the shelf. No money meant no shoes.

I wandered around for a while until Trey found me looking at shirts in Sparkeez Teez.

"Let's go," he said. "I gotta work in an hour."

I ignored him until he punched me in the shoulder.

"Come on, Joey, I gotta go."

I scowled at him. I didn't want to go home. I didn't want to ride in his junky car. I didn't want to admit I was jealous that he had a girlfriend. That he was old enough to have a job and his own money.

"Just go," I snapped. "I don't care what you do."

Those were the last words I said to him. Angry words. And I can't help wondering if he was still mad at me when he died.

I hope not.

CHAPTER
2

I don't know how you are supposed to
act when someone close to you dies.
Everyone seems to do it differently. Mom
went into a walking coma. Dad went to work.
Jayna bawled her head off at the funeral, her
boyfriend swiftly, tragically dead. High school
kids, parents, old people, cousins, grandparents,
teachers, coaches, and family friends filed
through the funeral chapel like zombies infected
with a sympathy virus.

What did they say? I don't remember. The
whole thing was a blur. I only remember a few
words from that whole week. Massive trauma.
Cerebral hemorrhaging. Life support. Dignified
death. Organ donation.

After the funeral, life went back to a twisted version of normal. On the outside, nothing really changed—except for the now-empty bedroom—but on the inside, everything was different.
I went back to school so numb that I barely noticed the weird stares kids gave me or the pats on the shoulder from "understanding" teachers. The counselor actually called me into her office to ask how I was doing.

How am I doing? I thought dizzily. I had no idea, so I shrugged and said, "Fine."

Her offer to make an appointment to talk barely registered in my brain. She said something about grief and slid a pamphlet across the desk that's still crammed into the bottom of my backpack.

Everyone is understanding, but no one understands.

✦ ✦ ✦ ✦ ✦

After school, before Mom and Dad would get home, I liked to go into Trey's room. Nothing had been moved except the dirty laundry. Mom had picked it up and washed it and put it back into his dresser—for what, I don't know.

His electric guitar still stood in its stand next to his desk, and an amplifier sat on the other side. Trey's laptop was still open on his desk. He'd been playing and mixing his own music for about a year. I would sneak in and listen sometimes when he was gone. He'd actually gotten pretty good.

I once asked Trey how hard it was to learn to play guitar. "Not bad," he said. "All you need is three chords and a beat." Then he ripped out a couple of bars of "Lock the Gates," his favorite song by his favorite band, Quake.

Now I was alone in his room. I didn't need to sneak anymore. I could look around as much as I wanted.

In the quiet, my mind jolted with an image of a big red pickup truck crossing the broken yellow line. It was heading straight for me. Straight for Trey. I'd heard descriptions of what happened. If I had been there, could I have screamed in time to warn him?

I shook the image from my mind as I grabbed Trey's music player off his nightstand and then ran back to my room. I plugged in my headphones and lay back on my pillow. A song by Quake started with an electronic hum that looped into a beat as the lead guitar kicked in. I imagined Trey playing, trying to learn the licks. I could almost hear his fingers fumbling on his guitar strings as he played and replayed the track.

I drifted off to sleep.

I woke when Mom called for dinner.

In my dreams, the big red pickup had been barreling down on us, about to run us over again.

CHAPTER
3

The fight that got me suspended wasn't even a fight. I shoved Raj Patel in the hallway because he poked me in the chest and laughed at my T-shirt.

It was wearing one of Trey's Quake concert T-shirts. He got it at a show last summer. I was wearing it because he would have worn it to school, but he wasn't there to do it.

"Hey, Fake!" Raj yelled and jabbed me with his finger.

Other guys laughed at his stupid joke, but I took it personally. I saw red and went after him. Raj was insulting my brother.

Raj's elbow slammed into a locker door. He claimed his shoulder was dislocated. He's not smart enough to know the difference between the tingling in his funny bone and the real agony of his shoulder socket coming apart.

Mr. Reynolds, the assistant principal, didn't see him start the fight. Instead of Raj getting in trouble for taunting, I got five days suspension. The only good part is that Raj cried a little, and the other guys made fun of him.

Dad had to come to school and meet with Mr. Reynolds over the whole thing. I sat in Mr. Reynolds' office waiting for my punishment. They'd never had to meet over any trouble with Trey.

"If it weren't for the other incidents I'd be inclined to let this one go," Mr. Reynolds told my dad.

I squirmed in my chair. I didn't like being in Mr. Reynolds' office. It was always bad news. And the look on his face got harder every time.

"But he hasn't been violent before," Dad said.

I wanted to say, "I wasn't violent this time, either! I just pushed the idiot!" But it only would have made things worse. So I did what I've gotten used to doing lately—sat there and kept my mouth shut.

"With Joey's anger issues, this is considered an escalation, and we can't let it go unanswered," Mr. Reynolds said.

They both looked at me, and I lowered my eyes. I wanted to crawl under the chair and stay there. At least being angry is better than feeling numb all the time. But they wouldn't understand that.

Mr. Reynolds leaned back in his chair. "I've discussed it with the counselors. We've seen some changes in Joey since Trey's passing, and we agree that . . ."

My dad stood up and wouldn't let him finish. "Thank you, Mr. Reynolds," he said quickly. "We'll deal with this at home."

The look on Mr. Reynolds' face was sheer confusion. How could the conversation be over? He wasn't finished telling my dad what was really wrong with me. But if I'd had a chance to talk to Mr. Reynolds alone, I could have explained that we don't talk about Trey. Never.

✦ ✦ ✦ ✦ ✦

On the ride home, we passed near the spot where my brother had his accident. I imagined the pillar of smoke rising over the tangle of metal. The crowd of police cars and fire trucks. The ambulance screaming away with a teenage boy. Doctors and prayers couldn't save Trey, but I knew I could have. Somehow. Only I wasn't there all because we'd had another one of our stupid fights.

✦ ✦ ✦ ✦ ✦

At the house, Dad made a sandwich for himself, grabbed a bag of chips, and then left to go back to work. A lecture would have been better than the unbearable silence of a dad who's angry and doesn't want to talk to you. But if we talked, Trey's name was bound to come up.

After he left, I tried numbing myself with TV, but there's nothing good on in the middle of the day. So I wandered the house awhile, knowing exactly where I would end up: Trey's room, staring at his guitar.

He'd kill me if I so much as touched it.

CHAPTER
4

Trey made playing guitar look easy, but with six strings and only four fingers—not including my thumb—I couldn't make the unwieldy thing put out a decent sound. Even when he fumbled through a song, my brother sounded way better than the mud I was pumping out.

I clamped the solid body of the guitar harder between my thigh and armpit, as if that would help. I also turned up the distortion, hoping it would make my musical mess seem less random, like the sounds I was making were done on purpose. I'm not sure if it helped at all, but at least my guitar playing filled the silence.

The tough thing about trying not to mention Trey at home was that almost all talking stopped. No one wanted to say anything that might make us think about or miss him. And if the tears started rolling, I knew that the accusation would come next. Mom and Dad never asked why I wasn't in the car with Trey on his drive home, but I'm sure they probably wonder, too, if that would have changed things.

I stopped playing for a moment and opened Trey's laptop. The screen came to life. I had five days to spend at home figuring out how to play guitar, and no Trey to help me, so it was up to online tutorials. I found dozens within seconds. The first one I found was how to play lead guitar on Quake's song "Lock the Gates." It was the same jam that Trey had played when he'd told me about three chords and a beat. I tried to follow along with the video, even got close on the first couple of notes, but it was way too hard.

I stopped for a minute, my heart sinking to my shoes. I felt in a weird way like I was failing Trey. Here I was in his room, at his computer, playing his guitar, and I couldn't even pull off a few notes.

I couldn't stop the tears once they started. I was glad that Mom and Dad weren't around. They would know why I was crying but would never ask if I was okay. Leaning over the guitar, I hung my head and sobbed.

I imagined Trey sitting next to me, not doing or saying anything, just watching. It hurt so bad in my gut and stuffed my head with so much misery that I now knew why I hadn't cried before, why Mom and Dad didn't cry—because this kind of pain felt like it would crush you.

As my breath started coming back, the flow of tears slowed. I hoped it was over. An alert sounded on the computer and startled me. I wiped my eyes and saw the video chat icon bouncing on Trey's computer screen. I looked around as if I were violating someone's privacy— add it to my list of felonies—and then clicked on the icon.

A childish part of my brain—the part that still wishes I could believe in Santa and the

Easter Bunny and the Tooth Fairy—expected to see Trey's face staring back me. Instead Jayna, Trey's girlfriend, appeared, filling the screen.

Her eyes were hopeful and hungry, mirroring my feelings—maybe Trey would show up on her screen. She tried to hide the disappointment, but I didn't take it personally.

"Oh . . . hi, Joey." Her brown eyes were kind and sad.

I looked at the clock in the corner of the screen. It was 3:30. School was out, and she was at home.

"Hi, Jayna."

"I saw that Trey was online, and I . . ." She stopped herself from admitting to her crazy hope and shifted gears. "What's up?"

I shrugged and lifted the guitar into view of the camera.

Her eyes went wide and then narrowed again. She smiled as a substitute for crying. "You play?"

I didn't know what made me do it, but I said, "Yeah, a little."

"Play me something?"

I went cold. I'd only been playing guitar for a few hours, and she was asking me for my first performance. But she was sad. She had logged on wanting to see Trey and got me instead. She needed to hear something, and I didn't want to disappoint her.

I set my fingers in the open G-chord arrangement I had learned 45 minutes earlier and dragged the plastic pick down the row of strings. The noise that came out of the amp was something like a guitar sound, so I strummed a couple more times before shifting to the C chord. My fingertips dragged clumsily across the strings as I changed notes, turning the sound sour. I tried not to let it stall me as I shifted to D for a couple of strokes, then back to G.

I played that progression a couple of times, tapping my foot as I went. I tried to hold the last note and let it ring like Trey would, but my fingers were tired and let up early, abruptly muting the strings.

I looked up at the screen. Jayna smiled back proudly.

"That's pretty good," she said. "You should be in a band."

My face burned with embarrassment, but for some reason that my stupid brain couldn't explain, I believed her.

CHAPTER
5

My first day back at school after my suspension, I heard some interesting rumors in the hallway—rumors, finally, that weren't related to Trey. Michael Xavier had a DJ show coming up—his first real gig. He had done school dances and the music for some of the assemblies. He was good, always matching his mixes to the mood. He'd done the music for Trey's memorial service at the school and really made it special. His pep rallies were the best—fun and rowdy—so I had no doubt he could do a full-scale show.

It was going to happen somewhere downtown, a big rave. Michael knew the neighborhood because he'd lived near there until last summer. Then he moved and came to our school. I wondered how the suburbs could be anywhere near as interesting, but he seemed to like it here.

Everybody was talking big, like they were going to his show. I wondered how many of them would actually make it. I wanted to be there too. Would Mom and Dad even notice if I disappeared for a night?

I took my seat in second-period history, right across the aisle from Michael. "Hey, MX," I said casually. He liked to be called by his DJ name.

"Joey Madden!" he announced in mock surprise. "Where have you been, man?"

I shrugged. Everyone knew that I'd been suspended and why.

MX waved a hand. "Aw, Patel, man," he groaned. "Kid's got a big mouth. He's not worth it."

I felt a connection with MX now, as artists — he was a DJ, and I was kind of a musician.

"Hey, MX, is it true? You have a gig?"

Actually, I was a little jealous. I wished I was a good enough musician put on a show like that.

MX chewed on the end of his pen and nodded.

"Yeah, in the old neighborhood, a place called the Concrete Gallery."

"Gallery?" I asked, imagining framed paintings on walls and weird-shaped sculptures on stands.

"It's really just a huge old warehouse by a rail yard where there's a bunch of graffiti. Great place for a show. But . . ." He shook his head, annoyed.

"Something wrong?" I asked.

He shrugged. "Kind of. I had an opening act. A funky techno-guitar group that would have been perfect to warm things up. But they bailed on me."

"You're not a headliner unless you have an opener," I said—something I'd heard in one of the guitar videos.

MX locked eyes with me. "I didn't think of it like that, but . . . yeah." His disappointment deepened.

I thought about Trey, about me playing his guitar, about an audience that would listen, and a crazy idea came into my head. I swept the classroom with my eyes and leaned closer to MX. "I'll . . . open for you."

He pulled his head back in surprise and stared at me.

"I . . . play guitar," I stuttered. "I'm starting a band, and we need a gig."

MX nodded and pointed his pen at me. "Your brother played, right?" He asked it without the dripping sympathy I usually hear when people talk about Trey. I was grateful for MX's way of asking about him.

I nodded. "Your gig is in three weeks?"

"Yep, Friday the eleventh," MX said.

I arched one eyebrow as if to ask, "Well?"

He pointed the pen at me again and smiled. "Okay, you got it," he said. "They're setting up the sound system, but you have to bring your own amps. How much time do you want?"

I froze, realizing he was asking something I didn't know how to answer. "Um . . ." I probably should have told him right then that I didn't have a band yet, and that I could only play two and a half songs, kind of. "A half hour?" I lied.

"Cool," MX said. "But I can't pay you."

I shrugged. "That's fine. That's not why I'm doing it."

CHAPTER
6

Carla Wallace played keyboards for the jazz band. She was pretty good—I think. I couldn't play the stuff she was playing. It sounded pretty complicated. But it was jazz, and even if I didn't understand it, it seemed like she knew what she was doing. So she's the first person I asked to join my band.

I caught up with her outside the cafeteria after lunch. She jumped a little when I touched her arm, not expecting anyone to tap her on the shoulder, even in the crowded hallway. Carla was shy and also more than a year older than most ninth graders. She'd been held back a grade or two in elementary school and seemed self-conscious about it.

When she looked at me with those
suspicious blue eyes, I almost lost my nerve. We'd
been lab partners in biology last year, so I kind of
knew her. If I didn't have that basic connection, I
never would have had the guts to talk to her. But
this was important.

"I play guitar," I said as if it were the right
thing to lead with. "I'm putting together a band
and I . . . like the way you play." I lifted both
hands palms down in front of me and wiggled
my fingers, like our language had no word
for *keyboard*.

Carla glanced around as if looking for this
band I was talking about. "What kind of music?"
she asked.

Quake played rock, so I shrugged and said,
"Rock, I guess."

She shook her head. Not knowing me very
well, she must have had little confidence in my
musical chops. "I don't think so. I'm kind of busy
with . . ."

"Kenny Miller is playing drums for us," I
blurted.

"Really?" Carla's eyebrows arched. The shyness evaporated for just a second, and a kind of wonder flickered in her eyes.

I nodded. Kenny was drum captain of the school marching band, and the rumor was that Carla had a bit of a crush on him. Kind of diabolical to use such information this way, but I was desperate. And Kenny and I did sort of know each other.

Carla tilted her head. "I didn't know you and Kenny were friends."

"Oh, yeah, we go way back," I said. It wasn't a complete lie. We'd been buds since grade school. But shortly after Trey's death, when my anger became a little more difficult to control, I told him to get out of my face, or else. I can't even remember why—not that it had to be a big reason at the time. We hadn't talked since.

Carla's gaze shifted. She got a distant look as if she was thinking about something more than just music.

Quickly I added, "We're meeting Thursday at my house. Got the garage to ourselves."

Carla bit her lip and calculated.

"What time?"

CHAPTER

7

I raced through the hallways to catch
Kenny at his locker. The marching band
had special lockers next to the band and choir
rooms—something about having to lug heavy
instruments around.

Kenny was just opening his locker and
dropping books inside when I saw him.

"Kenny!" I called. "Hey, Kenny!"

He eyed me as I jogged to a stop in front of
him. He didn't say anything, but "Why do you
suddenly want to talk to me?" was written all
over his face.

Magazine cutouts of rock drummers
were pasted on the inside of his locker door. I

recognized Bobbie Blitz from Quake, his big Afro fanning over his head as he hammered the drums in front of him.

"Hey, man, how's it going?" I asked casually, trying to catch my breath.

"Fine," Kenny said flatly. "What's going on? Did someone . . ." He stopped short of saying "die" but we both knew what he meant.

I waved it off, forgiving his mistake, and took the opportunity to use his sympathy to my advantage. "I'm starting a band." I pointed to the collage of drummers over his shoulder. "A rock band. To honor my brother."

He blinked a couple of times. "You don't . . ."

"I play guitar," I said. "Just started, but I'm decent. I had all last week to learn a few songs."

Kenny held back a laugh. "A week?"

It was a sharp insult. He didn't know how hard I'd worked that week. My anger rose, but I stuffed it back down. I couldn't blow up on him. Even an argument would get me kicked out of school again. And I needed Kenny's help.

"I'm not too bad. Three chords and a beat," I said.

He frowned, trying to guess the meaning of that statement.

"Something Trey used to say," I explained.

It must have been sophisticated enough to connect with a real musician, because Kenny's vibe changed. I suddenly had a little bit of respect from him. "Who else is playing with you?"

"Carla Wallace on keys."

The look in his eyes went all mushy at the mention of Carla's name. Without a word, I could tell he had a thing for her too. Perfect.

Kenny nodded vaguely. But I still saw some doubt in his eyes, and I wanted to erase it.

"It's going to be awesome, man. We're meeting Thursday after school at my house. You remember where it is?"

He kept nodding. "Who's playing bass?" he asked.

My face went blank. I didn't know we needed a bass player.

"Ask Vincent Black," Kenny offered.

I squinted at him. "Vincent plays bass?"

"Yeah, and he's pretty good—if you can deal with his weirdness."

My stomach sank. I would have to do a lot of convincing—and maybe some apologizing— to get Vincent to join my band. But maybe this was a worthy cause.

CHAPTER
8

Vincent Black, known on official school records as Vincent Blake, lived in an apartment with his mom near the freeway. I begged the secretary in the school office for his address. I promised her it was only about starting a band and that nothing bad would come of it. She was a nice lady who'd seen me in there too many times for the wrong reasons. I guess she was glad I was doing something constructive for a change and gave me the address.

At the apartment building, the second-floor hallway smelled like dinnertime—baking chicken and melted cheese. Televisions and voices chattered behind closed doors. I thought

I should make this quick and get home. Also, being late for dinner gave me an excuse to bail out if things went bad.

I knocked on the door and waited, expecting His Darkness, Vincent Black, to appear. But when the lock snapped and the door swung open, I was not prepared to see the small blonde woman standing in the doorway.

She looked like a normal mom, wearing slacks and a flowered shirt. She leaned her shoulder on the edge of the door. "Yes?" she asked politely.

"Uh . . . is . . . Vincent here?" I stammered, thinking somehow that I'd knocked on the wrong door.

She gave a tiny gasp of surprise. "Oh! You're here to see Vincent?"

Her reaction made me wonder how many guests Vincent ever had. There was a sense of happiness and hope in her face.

I nodded. "Yeah, I'm a friend of his." That's the longest stretch I'd made yet. But if it got me in the door, I was willing to lie a little bit to Mrs. Blake—or whatever her name was.

She swung open the door and smiled. "Come on in."

I followed her in and looked around. The apartment was neat and normal, not the black-threaded spiderweb I'd expected to walk into. She had dinner cooking on the stove.

"Vincent?" she called, stepping into the hallway, "You have a visitor." She turned and searched my face for an answer to an unasked question.

"Joey," I said helpfully.

"It's Joey," she said into the empty hallway.

The first door on the left popped open and swung inward a few inches with a lazy creak of the hinges.

"Well . . ." Vincent's mom said gently. She gestured to the door and left me for the kitchen.

I looked through the foot-wide crack in the door. The bedroom was shadowy and dim. "Vincent?"

"Enter," came a voice.

I nudged the door open and stepped in. Vincent was a shadow standing in front of the window, shades drawn against the afternoon sun and dark sheer curtains filtering the light even more. It was the black spiderweb I'd expected.

He raised his arms like he was conjuring smoke from the carpet. "Welcome to the Black zone."

CHAPTER
9

A glance around gave me the entire story of Vincent Black. Posters of rock bands covered every square inch of wall space and the ceiling. His bed sat against one wall, made up with a black-and-white checked bedspread. A desk stood along the opposite wall, cluttered with papers and textbooks and fiction novels with castles and dragons on the covers.

Vincent wore black jeans, black boots, and a long-sleeved black shirt. The black leather jacket he usually wore to school was absent. I almost chuckled, as I thought about how his mother probably made him hang it up in the closet when he walked in the door. The black fingernail polish and black eyeliner he always wore at school were present though.

Beside the desk, a long-necked electric bass guitar leaned against an amplifier. Two lights on the control panel glowed red. He'd just been playing. Cords snaked from the bass to the amp to a foot pedal distortion box to his laptop computer sitting atop the mess on his desk. A pair of headphones plugged into the computer hung over the arm of his office chair.

I recognized the sound-mixing program running on the screen—it was the same one Trey used. Desperate to make a connection, I pointed to the computer screen. "Band Jam. Good program."

"You use it?" Vincent asked in disbelief.

I shrugged. "Well, my brother did." I felt the need to keep him talking, open the connection a little more. "He played rhythm and lead guitar. Recorded some of his own stuff. I just started."

The mention of my dead brother caused Vincent to tip his head back and narrow his eyes at me.

"Why have you come?" he asked in a very official tone.

"I heard you play bass." I nodded to his instrument and amplifier. "I'm starting a band, and we need a bass player."

Vincent's reaction surprised me. He dropped his chin and looked away from me like I'd just hurt his feelings.

I didn't say anything for a second. Didn't want to antagonize him.

He sat down in his chair and reached for the bass, dragging it in front of him and setting it on his knee like a shield. "I don't work or play well with others." He plucked a couple of strings and held the note. I could hear the low hum emanate from the headphones. "My report cards say so." He looked up at me and hit me with the words I was dreading. "Besides, you haven't exactly been kind to me."

I slouched and nodded. He was right. He came to our school last year, already full Goth, already who he was, and I'd pointed and laughed at him in the hallway. I wouldn't have had the guts to come to a new school dressed like that. Maybe that's why I made fun of him.

I sighed. "You're right. I haven't been nice to you."

"You get in fights too," he reminded me, which was totally unnecessary. "You might try to beat me up."

I squinted at him. "I wouldn't—"

He cut me off. "You don't know what it's like, coming to a new school, being like . . ." He glanced down at himself.

I wanted to say, "Hey, you chose to be a freak! It's not my fault you get picked on!" But I held my tongue. This was going badly, and I couldn't let my anger get the best of me. Not now. I thought about pulling the ripcord and using my late-for-dinner excuse. But I couldn't. The clock was ticking, MX's show was only getting closer, and I couldn't leave here without a bass player. I decided to play the card I thought would appeal most to a guy who'd changed his name to Vincent Black.

"It's just that I have a gig already," I said shyly. "I want to do it in honor of my dead brother." Maybe throwing in the word dead was a little too obvious, but I was desperate.

Vincent studied me a long moment. "I've heard that the spirits of the suddenly dead hang around trying to figure out what happened to them."

The thought chilled me a bit. I pictured a vapor of Trey standing by his demolished car, watching the steam and the smoke rise, seeing the turned-over truck that had just collided with him, and thinking, *What happened?*

"I suppose," I said, not really knowing what to say. "I mean, I just want to do something to honor him since I feel somewhat guilty about what happened."

I wasn't sure where that bit of honesty came from, but Vincent didn't seem to be a person who had much patience for anything else.

"You didn't kill him, did you?"

The question was like a slap in the face. If it wasn't for the fact that I had accused myself of that once or twice, I would have done worse to Vincent than I had done to Raj Patel.

"No," was all I said. But I could never say it convincingly, not even to myself.

Vincent stared deep into my eyes in a way that made me uncomfortable. I suddenly really did want to bolt. But I needed this too much. This band and the show to honor Trey.

Vincent looked down and plucked a fat string on his bass. A sad minor note hummed in the headphones. "My dad died when I was a baby," he said. "I never knew him."

Now I understood why he was even willing to talk to me, a kid who'd tormented him in the past. He really was searching for something. Maybe to know whether his dad was around and cared about him. I began to think that maybe all of this was too sad, too heavy, that maybe neither of us could handle forming a band dedicated to a dead boy.

"Who are you covering?" he asked. This was a question he'd ask only if he was planning to join us.

I took a hopeful breath and looked at his posters. I found one showing the cover of Quake's third album, *Shattertown*, one of Trey's favorites. "Quake, for sure. And whoever else we want." Before he could think about it any longer, I said, "Thursday after school. My house. I'll text you the address."

I turned to leave.

"Wait," Vincent said.

I froze, worried he was already changing his mind. He'd done the quick calculation and realized he'd just agreed to spend hours outside his spider den of darkness and hang with other people.

But he didn't say forget it. Instead he asked, "What's the band's name?"

I stood there and contemplated the reason I was doing this. I imagined the last moment of Trey's life, there on the road, the thing that really killed him, the big red pickup truck racing toward his car.

I glanced at Vincent over my shoulder. "Speed," I said surely, as if it had been the idea all along.

In the corner of my eye, I could see him nod. "See you Thursday."

CHAPTER
10

I didn't know how good Carla and Kenny and Vincent were—and exactly how bad I was—until all four of us were together in my garage Thursday. By 4:00 I had Trey's guitar and amplifier set up and was ready for the other three.

Kenny's dad dropped him off, and I helped him carry his drums—way fewer than I thought he'd bring—from their van. A couple of minutes later, Carla pulled her little red hatchback up to the curb with her keyboard, stand, and amp in the back. The car was dented and scratched and a little rusty in spots, but it got her and her instrument here, so I didn't care.

Vincent was last to show up. He rode an
old-style cruiser bicycle—black, of course—with
wide-set handlebars, big metal fenders, and a
fake gas tank on the crossbar. His bass was in a
soft case attached to two shoulder straps slung
over his back, the neck sticking way up over his
head like a flagpole. He carried a small amplifier
on a rack over the back fender.

They set up quickly and we started to jam,
just playing notes and rhythm with no particular
song in mind. I knew I was in over my head
right away.

Kenny had brought only three drums,
which he named for me—a snare that he leaned
over and struck to get that *snap* in the rhythm, a
lower-toned tom on a stand next to it, and a big
floor tom standing to his right. He also brought
one ride cymbal that he could tap to the beat or
crash for punctuation. He had a whole bunch
more drums at home, he said, but this was a
stripped-down set that he could easily move.

Also, he didn't sit down. He stood among
his drums and played. It looked nothing like

a typical rocker's drum kit. But the floor tom thumped deeply like a kick bass when he hit it, and it all worked. The guy really was good.

Vincent fell into a groove easily with Kenny. He followed the beat and added deep notes from the bass. He didn't look at anyone as he played. He seemed to be having a private conversation with his instrument.

Carla rolled into a jazzy kind of keyboard playing with sweet notes and a lot of flourishes. She held the melody really well, which was good, because I was a disaster.

I tried playing the open chords I'd learned on the Internet videos, but it was hard to hit all the strings right when someone else set the beat. I fumbled my changes, dragging my fingertips across the strings as I searched for the next note. I accidentally pressed the strings to the front of the frets instead of the back, blanking out the sound. The plinking noise echoed out of my amplifier and ratcheted up my frustration.

My bandmates adjusted, slowing down the beat and sticking to the three chords I knew—G,

C, and D. It helped, but after half an hour my left hand got tired and sore from pressing on the strings, and I fell behind again.

I looked around helplessly, only to see Carla and Kenny making eyes at each other as they played. It was my first suspicion that their attraction, which had helped me get them both in my band, could eventually become a problem.

Vincent reached over and touched my shoulder. "You know power chords?"

I nodded. I'd seen some demoed on the Internet.

"Play those instead," he suggested.

A power chord only required me to play two strings at a time. I set my fingers on the fretboard and pressed my index finger on the top string and my ring finger on the next one down, leaving one fret open between them. Sliding my hand up and down the guitar's neck, I could play a lot more notes. The sound wasn't as rich, but the melody was there.

I smiled gratefully at Vincent. He nodded and went back to meditating with his bass.

CHAPTER
11

We jammed for an hour and a half,
dropping into a few familiar melodies
that sounded like songs we knew, but
not really trying to play a whole tune. I
still struggled and fumbled, but what I was doing
sounded like music at least.

At 5:30, my mom's car pulled into the
driveway, and I waved everyone quiet. She got
out of her car, her purse slung over one shoulder
and her soft briefcase hanging from the other.

"What's going on?" she asked, a little bit of
amusement showing on her face.

"Band practice," I said.

She stared at me for a long moment, surprise hanging between us. She and Dad didn't know I'd started playing. I wasn't exactly hiding it from them, but the reason I'd never mentioned it came next.

She looked from my face to Trey's guitar hanging around my neck, and her expression went cold. "Okay," she muttered without looking at me, then walked toward the front door.

Carla, Kenny, and Vincent stared at me, frozen. Their collective look asked if we were all in trouble.

I waved my hand. "It's cool. Don't worry about it. But we should probably quit for the day. Meet again Saturday?" I asked them.

Kenny and Carla exchanged glances. Carla blushed. "Sure," she said, and Kenny nodded.

"That is agreeable," Vincent mumbled, and he started breaking down his equipment.

Carla loaded her stuff into her car and offered Kenny a ride home. I told Kenny it was okay to leave his drums because we kept the garage locked.

"Oh, hey, before you leave . . ." I grabbed a short stack of pages off my amp, printouts of the list of songs I wanted to play.

The band looked through the set list, glanced at each other, and then looked at me.

"You want to play these?" Kenny asked.

I nodded. But inside I was shaking with nerves.

Carla squinted at me. "You're going to learn all of these in three weeks?"

"There's only six," I explained. "I can do it."

Carla and Kenny shrugged and found pockets for my set list. Vincent said nothing.

Carla and Kenny drove off, and I felt a sense of pride that I'd helped bring them together, and jealousy because I kind of liked Carla too. But nothing worth breaking up the band over.

Vincent, with his black eyeliner and crazy black hair, sat on his bike in my driveway.

"Practice those chords," he said simply.

It was a bit of a warning. He wasn't happy with my playing, but he wasn't dismissing me either. There was a little bit of encouragement there.

I nodded and took the guitar and amplifier back to Trey's room, where it belonged.

CHAPTER
12

Supper that night was especially tense. Mom was rattled by seeing me with Trey's guitar. Dad asked about the drum set in the garage.

"It's—" I started to explain, but Mom cut me off.

"Joey has a band," she said flatly. She was trying to keep the hurt out of her voice, but she wasn't succeeding.

Dad looked at me in surprise. "You play . . . ?"

I opened my mouth, but Mom answered again. "Guitar."

He looked from me to her, then down at his plate. "Oh."

I took the opportunity to say something in the silence. "We have a show in three weeks."

Dad nodded at his mashed potatoes. "Using Trey's guitar."

What was that tone—betrayal?

I poked at the chicken on my plate. Something bubbled deep inside me, hot like lava. Whatever it was, I couldn't describe it, couldn't say it to these people.

"I'm not hungry," I muttered. I left the table and went to my room.

I tried to do homework, but reading and doing math are hard when your thoughts are drowned out by anger and shame. I was soaked with the feeling that Trey's death was just wrong, and that somehow Mom and Dad thought I was responsible. Maybe they were right. I wasn't where I was supposed to be when it happened. I refused to leave the mall with Trey that day because I was . . . being me. And I survived.

After an hour of staring at the same textbook page and making no progress, I cracked open my door and listened to the house. The TV chattered in the family room, and dishes clattered in the kitchen. Mom and Dad were both distracted.

I went into the hallway and ducked into Trey's room. I closed the door, sat down in Trey's chair, turned on the amplifier, and plugged in the headphones.

I sat there for a while strumming and sliding my fingers along the frets. It sounded good, felt good. I played until I cried and kept playing. I don't even know what time I went to bed. The house was silent when I slipped out of his room and back into my own.

CHAPTER
13

The next three weeks went great,
despite a few clumsy notes by me on
Trey's guitar. I practiced alone every minute
I could and started keeping up with Carla,
Kenny, and Vincent when we played together.
I still only felt comfortable with my three
chords—G, C, and D—but I figured I should
stick with what I could play. I downloaded lyrics
for the songs and sang as we played, but I didn't
have a microphone, so I really had no idea how
my voice sounded.

We changed the set list that I'd handed out
the first day of practice. The others were right—
it was way too ambitious. The list we ended up
with was a group of songs I could play with my

limited chords, and that the other three could embellish with their skills. Two of the songs were Quake hits.

I was worried everyone would get bored with my limited abilities, but no one complained. Their loyalty was helped by the fact that Carla and Kenny could spend time together, and Vincent got out of the house and did something with other people which got his mom off his back.

As the big day approached, there was a lot of buzz in the ninth-grade hallway about MX's show. People promised rides to each other and arranged sleepovers to cover their tracks if the night went late.

MX announced that he had an opening act. When people asked who, he mentioned my name. That accounted for the weird looks I was getting in the hallways. No one believed I was capable of putting a band onstage for a full set. Ah, well, I'd show them—I hoped.

✦ ✦ ✦ ✦ ✦

The disaster started first thing Friday morning. I hadn't heard from Kenny since our Tuesday practice. I couldn't get him by phone or text or catch him in the hallway. His drum kit sat silent during our Thursday session since he didn't show up. I was mad because it was our last rehearsal.

I went to his locker Friday morning and waited. Kenny showed up five minutes before first period and slouched when he saw me there.

"Where have you been, man?" I held my anger back, but my nerves were driving me nuts.

Kenny shook his head and dialed his locker combination. He wouldn't look me in the eye.

"I can't go."

I gaped at him, not wanting to believe that he was talking about the show.

"My dad found out where it is, in that part of town. It's dangerous there, you know." He took a book from his locker and then closed it.

"You can't back out, Kenny. We have a gig, and we need you." I slammed my fist against the locker next to his to punctuate my seriousness.

He looked down at the floor. I expected to see frustration in his face, anger at his dad for not letting him go. Instead, he seemed to accept the situation.

"It's a bad part of town," he repeated. "Maybe another time."

He walked off.

I stood there as the world crumbled under my feet. My mind was frozen. I couldn't begin to think how to fix this.

The first bell rang and unfroze me. I couldn't be late for class or it would mean trouble for my record. I ran to class, took my seat in time for roll call, and sat there panicking in my chair. No beat, was all I could think. We need three chords and a beat, and now we have no beat!

✦ ✦ ✦ ✦ ✦

I found Carla near the music hallway. "You good for tonight?"

"Yeah," she said, but she didn't sound so sure.

"I know Kenny can't make it, but we can still do the show." I was thinking fast now. "We need this . . . to be a real band . . . to get more gigs. Six o'clock at my house?"

She gave a shrug and nodded.

Good enough.

"I'll see you . . . at six," I said.

✦ ✦ ✦ ✦ ✦

Before school was out, I found Vincent hanging out in the courtyard with some other Goth kids. All of them looked surprised when I just walked up and started talking to him.

"We're still on for tonight, right?"

He stared back at me a long moment.

"Kenny quit, didn't he?"

"No. He's still in the band. He just can't play this gig."

"Sounds like quitting to me," Vincent said.

I couldn't contain my temper anymore. My face went hot, and I stuck my finger in his face.

"You promised. You said it was a good idea and that you'd play."

He leaned away from my anger.

"You going to beat me up if I don't?"

His black-clad friends circled around me as I took a breath and tried to bring some sense to my brain. Things would only end badly for me, so I either had to stop before my anger got the best of me or forget about honoring Trey.

"No, I'm not . . . Look, I have a lot on the line here. I need this . . . we need this gig. Carla's still in. Are you? I need to know."

Vincent nodded. "I made a vow," he said formally. "I will honor it."

I left, disaster 75% averted.

CHAPTER
14

Vincent rolled up to my garage on his bike a few minutes early, bass on his back and amp on the fender. We didn't say much while we waited, and I got the vibe that he was a little mad about me getting in his face earlier. I thought about apologizing but didn't know what to say. Bandmates fight sometimes, I figured. We'd get over it.

Carla got there at 6:00 sharp. A trail of blue smoke clouded around the back of her little red hatchback as she pulled into the driveway. She turned off the engine and got out.

"Your car okay?" I asked, pointing to the blue mist behind it.

She waved her hand like she was shooing a fly. "It's been doing that all week. It's fine."

She acted irritated, and I didn't have to wonder what the problem was. She'd expected to do this show with Kenny, but now it was just her and us two weirdoes minus a drummer.

"We're on in an hour and a half," I said, trying to push some authority. Someone had to be in charge of this band, and I'd gotten us together, so I guessed that someone was me. "Let's load up."

We squeezed Trey's guitar and amp in around Carla's keyboard and gear. Vincent's stuff was harder to get in. We had to fold down the backseats, leaving no place for a third person to sit. I'd already irritated these two, so I volunteered to take whatever space was left in back for the drive downtown.

I crawled in behind the passenger seat and lay awkwardly across the folded seats, propping myself up on one elbow.

As Carla backed out of the driveway, I glanced at the front of the house. Mom and Dad didn't come out to say good luck. I knew they somehow felt betrayed by what I was doing, but it hurt.

CHAPTER

15

Disaster struck again on Washington Avenue at the edge of downtown. We'd just gotten off the freeway when Carla's car started sputtering. She stopped for a red light, and when it turned green, the car would barely move. It sped up for half a block, then slowed down again. She kept stomping on the gas pedal as if it would help. I looked behind us and was alarmed by the cloud of blue smoke trailing us.

"Hey," I said, "something's seriously wrong. Are we on fire?"

Carla pulled over in front of a dingy storefront, and we piled out of the car. The smoke was clearing, but the cloud rising from under the back bumper drew some attention from people on the sidewalk. The world was collapsing again.

I pulled out my cell phone and looked at the clock. "We only have an hour to get there," I said. We'd had plenty of time to make it to the gallery and set up. Now we were going to be late.

"I have to call my sister," Carla said.

"Your sister will drive us?" Vincent asked.

She shook her head. "No. This is too much for me."

"What?!" I screeched. The word echoed back to me in the urban canyon.

"She goes to the university right over there," Carla said, pointing beyond the buildings across the street. "She can come and pick us up."

"We're on in an hour, Carla," I reminded her. "We have a set. MX is waiting. They're all waiting!"

"I'm not even supposed to be going," she said.

Vincent and I exchanged a curious glance.

Carla sighed. "I told my mom I was doing jazz practice tonight. She'd never let me come downtown for some rave." The last word came out in a sneer, like she was disgusted with the idea of playing a wild dance party. Kenny's last-minute cancellation only made her decision now easier. "I'll get us back home, I promise."

It was a promise I didn't want.

She slid her phone out of her pocket, pressed a couple of buttons, and held it to her ear. "Hey, it's me."

I didn't hear the rest of her conversation—didn't have to. She was quitting, ditching us. I stepped off the curb and to the back of her car. I lifted the hatchback and grabbed my guitar in its soft case, then got my amplifier. The thing was bulky and heavy. I wished I had a small one like Vincent's.

"What are you doing?" Carla asked as she ended the call to her sister.

I looked into the sliver of sky above our heads. The sun was going down.

"I have a gig to play. Said I'd be there at 7:30."

On the surface, I was trying to be all business, but I could hear the quaver in my voice—anger, always just under the surface, ready to come out.

"Joey, don't be mad," she said.

I clenched my jaw so hard it hurt. "I'm not mad," I hissed. I slung the guitar over my back and hefted the amp.

"I still want to be in the band," Carla pleaded.

I didn't look at her as I stalked off in the direction of our gig.

CHAPTER
16

"Joey!" Vincent called from half a block behind.

I turned and saw him trotting toward me, bass guitar towering over his head and his little amp swinging in his right hand. It was a surprising sight. I figured he would catch a ride back to the suburbs with Carla's sister. Maybe I would have done the same if I thought I had an option. But here he was, chasing after me.

"Don't blame her, man, she's nervous is all."

I looked past him and could see Carla's car several blocks back. She was handing equipment to another girl, her sister, who was putting it in the backseat of another car.

"She got here fast," I said. It was almost an accusation.

Vincent frowned, burning me with disapproval. "Not everything has to be a fight, you know."

My face got hot, so I changed the subject. "I didn't think you were coming."

He shrugged. "I couldn't leave her there alone. Bad neighborhood."

I nodded and turned away. I didn't want him to see the shame in my eyes. I had left Carla on an unfamiliar and dirty street, surrounded by strangers, because of my short temper.

Vincent and I trekked along the sidewalk in silence. I knew the route to take because MX had given me directions, which I'd double-checked online. The neighborhood got more dingy and rough. After a couple of turns, we walked past a place called God's Corner, some kind of homeless shelter that MX had mentioned, so I knew we were in the right area.

Two blocks over, I saw trouble. Just when I thought the worst had already happened,

I spotted three kids standing on a corner a block away. They were a little older than Vincent and me, and all had long dreadlocks hanging down to their shoulders.

The skinny one with a red mop zeroed in on us first. He tapped the big one with dark dreads on the chest. Soon all three of them were staring at us. These guys were staking out a chunk of land and owning it. And they weren't going to let us through without paying a toll— or worse.

Vincent stiffened, and I immediately felt vulnerable. We were carrying expensive instruments that would be easy to sell at a pawnshop or a secondhand music store. I started calculating, hoping my anger would turn me into a monster that no one would mess with. But I really felt more scared than anything else.

Two more mop-heads appeared around the corner. We were way outnumbered now.

"Maybe we should cross the street," I muttered to Vincent.

"Uh-huh," he said.

I glanced at the corner opposite of where the five thugs stood and my stomach sank. Two more guys in dreadlocks appeared. Seven of them now. They had the end of the block sealed off.

I frantically looked for another option. There was an opening directly across the street from us, a slot in the buildings leading into a shadowy alleyway. But there was light at the other end—another street and maybe safety.

Without warning I made a left-hand turn and shouted, "Come on!" to Vincent.

I cut across traffic and got blasted by a car horn. I heard Vincent's feet thumping right behind me. Within seconds we were in the alley.

A shout echoed behind us. Probably Red, angry that his gang's easy targets were escaping.

On the brick wall, my eye caught a four-foot-tall tag in red and metallic blue— "DREAD7" in big bubble letters with a stick man hanging by the neck from the branch of the 7. I didn't have time to wonder if this was

the tag of the gang behind us. I was too busy
running for my life.

CHAPTER
17

The end of the alley couldn't come fast enough. My legs were already tired, and the amplifier was like a cement block I'd been cursed to lug everywhere I went. My shoulder stung from the weight, and its plastic handle cut into my palm. I thought about throwing it behind a trash bin so I could run faster, but it belonged to Trey. I wasn't going to give it up so easily.

When we hit the next sidewalk, Vincent was right on my heels, chugging air. The footfalls of the gang members chewed up ground behind us. I didn't know how much gas I had left in my tank. I might collapse any second and become a carcass for the vultures.

Thankfully my eyes found two things across the street that gave me a boost—a big building with a huge sign reading "TRANSIT STATION" and a police officer with a cell phone to his ear standing by the entrance.

Without looking, I ran into the street, Vincent in tow, just as a bunch of cars left the next intersection. I ignored the honking horns and sprinted for safety.

When my feet hit the other sidewalk, I almost cheered. Instead I stopped, bent over, and inhaled some thick city air. Vincent stood next to me, hands on hips, gasping.

I sat down on my amp, letting the rush of blood slow in my veins.

"I saw that," a man's voice accused.

I looked up. "Huh?"

The police officer appeared at my side.

"I could give you two tickets for jaywalking, you know," he said sternly.

I looked up at his face and recognized the expression. He was looking for a reason not to hassle us or have to do paperwork.

I pointed across the street. "But they were chasing us."

He followed my finger to the blank alley slot. No one was there. He glared back at me as if he'd caught me in a lie.

"Just be careful out here," he said and walked away.

Without a word, Vincent picked up his amp and headed for the entrance to the station.

"Hey, it's this way," I pointed up the street.

He just shook his head as he passed the cop and pushed the glass door open.

I grabbed my amp and lugged it behind him, avoiding the officer's eyes. Inside, Vincent stood looking up at a red LED sign that showed places and times—the bus schedule.

"We can still make it," I said. "We're only a few minutes away."

He shook his head slowly. I recognized defeat when I saw it.

"I'm out, man. This is too much."

My anger rose. I nudged him on the shoulder, harder than I meant to.

"You can't give up! We're almost there!"

He shied away from me and stared into my face, his black eyeliner blurry with sweat. He didn't like getting shoved and seemed afraid I would hit him.

The combination of our show evaporating and that look he gave me—like I was some kind of violent monster—made me explode.

"I can't believe you're quitting!"

He threw his shoulders up. "It's over, Joey! It's not happening!"

I took it as an insult and shot venom back at him.

"Coward!" I spat.

Vincent's eyes went cold. The fear and the fight left him. He turned to me slowly, face grim. "Why does everything have to be a fight with you?"

"Because life sucks!" I snapped. Heads turned in the crowd. I didn't care. "One day everything's okay, and the next day it's all messed up. Nobody keeps things right—just right, that's all I want, just for a while!"

He knitted his brow. "Is this about your brother?"

"The whole thing's about my brother!" I shouted. "I . . ."

My voice thickened in my throat, and the words wouldn't come. I simply could not say what I'd suspected for months—that Trey died because of me, that it was my fault. Maybe the extra five seconds I'd have taken fastening my seat belt before he pulled out of the parking space would have made the truck miss him on the road. Maybe I could have screamed, "LOOK OUT!" from the passenger's seat at just the right time. Or, if nothing else, maybe I would have died with him. That seemed more right, more just, than him just being gone.

Vincent's face read disgust and pity. Mostly pity.

"You're seriously messed up, man." He shook his head and walked off toward the bus garage. He'd be home in an hour. Safe.

I sat down on my amp and dropped my face into my hands.

CHAPTER
18

I sat there a long time, surrounded by blackness and misery and hurt. *Maybe I should buy a bus ticket and just go somewhere,* I thought, *anywhere. There must be a place where life is better, where everything doesn't hurt so much.*

Inside my pocket, my phone vibrated with an incoming text. I sighed and pulled it out. It was MX: *U close? Almost showtime!*

I stared at it a minute, frozen with indecision. Showing up alone would let him down. I'd promised him a band, not a single skinny kid with a guitar and no backup. I looked at the door to the garage. Another bus would be leaving for my neighborhood within 15 minutes.

I could just get on it and go home. No show. No band. No excuses.

Suddenly I heard Trey's voice. "All you need is three chords and a beat." I looked over my shoulder, half expecting to see his face staring down at me. But I knew it wasn't possible.

My phone buzzed in my hand. It was MX again: *????*

This time, I didn't ignore it. I opened the screen and texted back, *Almost there. CU in a few.*

I stood and picked up my amplifier. Trey's guitar hadn't left my back since Carla's car. I was carrying it like a life-support tank, and I wouldn't let it go. I passed the door to the bus garage and exited onto the street. I looked left and right—no speeding cars, no guys with dreadlocks.

My solo walk to the venue wasn't encouraging. The streetscape grew more grim. Brick buildings that once had been businesses sat empty and sad. But at least there weren't any people threatening me.

I got to the end of the long street, and even though it was dark, I found the hole in the fence easily. It was just as MX had described it. A guy and a girl were slipping through it.

"Hey," I called.

The guy stopped as the girl ducked through the fence.

"You guys going to the Gallery?" I asked.

"Yeah," he said, nodding at my guitar and amp. "You a musician?"

His girlfriend was standing inside the fence now, watching, a black baseball cap hooding her eyes.

I stepped into the street and headed straight for him. "Yep, I'm opening for MX. Can I walk with you guys?" I tried to keep the fear out of my voice. The truth is, the place looked like an industrial graveyard with ghosts and the whole works. Those two seemed comfortable with the shadows and the steel skeletons.

The guy held open the flap of fence and waved me forward. "Sure. Come on."

I bent and slipped through the fence hole, careful not to snag my guitar case on the crossbar.

When I stood up, the girl pointed at the guitar slung across my back.

"You been playing long?"

I shrugged. "A while." Not a lie.

The guy caught up with us and reached for my amplifier. "Need a hand?"

My first instinct was to slap his hand away, afraid he was trying to steal it. But my shoulder seriously ached, and I was glad for the help. I let him have it. How far could he run? We were all going to the same place.

I followed them into the dark rail yard as they pointed out some of the graffiti they'd written on boxcars. Their friendliness felt warm and safe.

CHAPTER
19

MX stood next to his equipment and stared at me. He had two turntables, his laptop, a mixer, a control board for lights, and two plastic bins of vinyl albums set up on a big table.

The sound system had already been set up. Stacks of big speakers bookended the small stage. Heavy wires ran everywhere, and a rainbow of lights flashed on every graffiti-covered wall in this huge open-air room.

And there I was with a guitar and an amplifier and nobody else.

"What's up?" MX asked. "Where's Kenny and Carla and . . ." he searched for the name.

"Vincent," I said, shaking my head. "They flaked."

He tried to make sense of it for a second, then said, "So you're going to, what, do a thirty-minute guitar solo?"

I didn't know what to say, how to convince him that there'd still be an opening act.

"Three chords and a beat," I said.

MX grimaced at me. "Huh?"

I pulled my guitar off my back and said, "I can play G, C, and D chords pretty well." I reached in my back pocket and slid out the list of songs that Speed was planning to play. "You know any of these songs?" I bit my lip, assuming that he only knew house music and techno.

He nodded. "Yeah, I know all of them."

I let out a grateful breath. "Can you give me a beat and some accompaniment? I can play rhythm and sing." I pointed to the mike he'd set up center stage.

MX squinted at the list. Then he looked up at me and smiled. "We're really going to suck."

I gave him an encouraging pat on the shoulder. "I trust you, man."

He nodded and left me for his pit. I went to center stage and looked out into the gathering crowd, everyone chattering excitedly at one another. No one noticed me. I got power to my amp, plugged my guitar into it, and connected the whole thing to MX's sound system. I found G and strummed a couple of times to check the sound. MX nodded and gave me a thumbs-up.

When I turned around, the entire crowd was staring up at me. I didn't recognize a single face. I wondered how many of those talkers at school who swore they were coming to the show had car trouble, or were afraid to come to this part of town, or were denied by their parents. Part of me wondered if I was even supposed to be here with these strangers.

My insides turned to jelly and my knees started shaking—not from running this time, but from a different kind of terror. MX must have hit a button on his control panel, because a white spotlight snapped on and blinded me. The crowd disappeared from my sight. I was grateful that I couldn't see them.

I blew into the microphone and heard my breath in the big speakers. Then I cleared my throat, hoping the knot would go away. It didn't. But I couldn't stand there all night. "Um . . . this one's for Trey," I finally said. My voice echoed off the walls and blended with the wild artwork all around.

I turned to MX and nodded. He hit a button and started a beat that sounded close to Quake's "Lock the Gates."

I hit the G chord and everything sounded perfect.

CHAPTER
20

Someone took video for MX and posted it. By Monday morning, everyone who'd said they'd be there had watched the show online instead. My opening set took up the first thirty minutes, and apparently people actually watched that too. I think Trey would have been proud of me.

I was getting high fives in the hallway, and some of the girls smiled shyly at me. A couple of guys said they liked the sound that MX and I had together. It was a bit unusual to have just a guitar backed by a DJ like that.

I didn't admit to anyone that I'd watched the video too—a couple of times. I agreed that we sounded pretty good. MX knew a lot about music, but putting together backing tracks like that on the spot really showed what an insanely amazing musician he was. I didn't like my singing. Maybe I could get better at it.

I had shyly called Mom and Dad to the computer for one viewing. They sat next to me, watching in silence. When my set ended, Mom was sniffling and left the room. Dad squeezed my shoulder, said, "That was great, Joey, but you probably should let us know the next time you plan on going to a neighborhood like that."

A few caring words, laced with a note of worry. It wasn't a parade, but I felt like something had changed between us. Everything was a little softer and more open.

Vincent found me by my locker and shrugged as he walked up to me. He didn't need to say anything. It was a crazy night. He seemed to be looking for forgiveness.

"I'm sorry," I said, not remembering the last time I'd actually said those words to anyone and felt it. "I melted down on you. I wouldn't have hurt you."

"I know," he said. "That was scary though. And a little bit awesome."

"Yeah, it was."

"I saw the video," Vincent said. "Really good. So does this mean we don't have a band anymore?"

I closed my locker and walked away into the crowd, Vincent at my side.

"Kenny and Carla are out," I said.

I'd texted them over the weekend, and they didn't want anything to do with a rock band that played at dumps. Plus, over the weekend they had figured out a way to get together without music as an excuse.

I'd made a lot of mistakes leading up to that show. But I didn't give up. I did it for Trey, and I think that has allowed me to forgive myself some. I will never know if I could have stopped him from dying that day, or if I would have just been another casualty. And thinking about it isn't going to help me move on. Playing music will, and it will also help me remember and honor Trey.

"I still want to play," Vincent said.

"Good," I said. "MX wants to do it again. I've got three chords, he's got the beat. But we need you. Because, to tell the truth, we need some rhythm too."

About the Author

Chris Everheart is a recovering reluctant reader turned award-winning author of books for young readers. His YA series The Delphi Trilogy has been described as "unputdownable," a thriller that even the most reluctant of readers will want to keep reading. When not writing, he can be found watching TV, reading fiction (and nonfiction), hiking in the mountains near his home, or visiting schools and libraries to share his love of learning. He lives in Tennessee with his family. You can learn more about him at www.chriseverheart.com.

Questions to Think About

1. Joey is inspired to take up guitar and play a show to honor his dead brother. What inspires you? Describe a person or event that pushed you toward trying something new. How were you inspired, and were you successful?

2. Imagine that you are Joey. What would you have done differently when Kenny said he couldn't play in the show? Do you think you could have kept the band together?

3. Joey feels guilty for his brother's death. Why? Do you feel he should? Have you ever felt the same way for something that wasn't entirely your fault?

THE 13TH FLOOR

Sam is happy to be included with the popular football players, who happen to play the same video game he does. When they get their hands on a pirated copy of *The 13th Floor*, a game banned for violence and gore, Sam gives it a try. Soon he and his friends find the game to be so hypnotic that they can't stop playing, even after it begins to take control of their real lives.

The Squadron

Sera has a chance to join an elite group of space pilots. All she needs to do is complete one flight, from the Old World to the New Colonies. But damage to one of her engines sends her off course. She crashes onto a violent dwarf planet with a molten core that is slowly devouring its surface. And that might be the least of her worries.

THE WISH

Before a fight with the strongest kid in school, Robert wishes for a miracle that would save his face from being turned into a bloody pulp and change everything about the world he lives in. When his wish is granted, Robert quickly learns that the new world it created comes with its own set of problems.